Ruby and Alfie Because We Love You

"For all of my wonderful dogs; those I have known and those I have yet to know.
And with thanks to Simon and Pete"

HARUKI Publishing

Haruki Publishing Copyright ©Hilary Gibb
ISBN 978-0-9571911-9-1

www.hilgibbauthor.co.uk

This is Ruby and Alfie. Ruby and Alfie are twins. They are mischievous,

shiny and have hearts of gold - just like you.

Ruby and Alfie like to...

...play imaginary games

...sing

...read

...run

...jump

...and write

...explore

Last Tuesday, Ruby and Alfie decided that they wanted to show their Mum just how much they really love her...

"I really love Mum," said Ruby.
"I really, really love Mum," said Alfie.

Pointing to his moon poster on the wall, Alfie said, "I love Mum to the Moon and back."

Stretching her arms out wide, Ruby said, "I love Mum to Mars and back."

"Look," said Ruby kindly. "We both know that we both really, really, really love Mum."
"To the Sun and back!" shouted Alfie, all excited.

Alfie announced, "I know! We could get Mum some really expensive, fantabulous jewellery to show how much we love her!"

Ruby tipped their piggy banks upside down. Two coins and a button fell out. "But we haven't got enough money," she said.

"How about some super trendy, glamorous shoes?" asked Alfie.

"Oh no," declared Ruby, giggling. "Mum always falls over in high heels!"

"What about a beautiful bird?" suggested Ruby.

"Mum loves watching nature programmes."

Alfie looked uncertainly at Dave. "I'm not sure what Dave would make of that."

"We could take Mum on an amazing jungle holiday," suggested Ruby.

"Hmmm..." thought Alfie out loud, "Mum really doesn't like snakes."

Getting a bit desperate for ideas, Alfie said, "What about performing some music for Mum?"

Ruby liked the idea, but looked doubtful. "Mum does love music, but we don't know how to play, yet."

"So," said Ruby, determined not to be beaten. "How about we bake Mum a magnificent cake?"

"Mmmm yummy," said Alfie. "But I'm not sure that we could get the cake into the oven."

Ruby and Alfie really wanted to show Mum just how much they loved her. But what could they do? They thought... and thought... and thought some more.

The twins strained their brains.

"I know!" Alfie exclaimed. "I know what we can do to make sure Mum sees just how much we love her!"

"What?" asked Ruby. Aflie explained, "We're so great at building sandcastles and we have loads of sand. And it won't cost us any money... So, let's build our best ever sandcastle for Mum!"

"That's the bestest idea ever Alfie," said Ruby. "But it's raining outside."

"That's not going to stop us," exclaimed Alfie.

Even though the sand was soaking wet, Ruby and Alfie busied themselves building a fantabulous castle for mum.

Ruby and Alfie brought Mum to come and see their sandcastle. They stood proudly next to their creation, looking very pleased with themselves.

The twins were very confused when Mum stared at their sandcastle with a horrified look on her face. "What have you done to our brand new carpet?!" howled Mum in despair. "In fact, why would you do this to any carpet?"

Ruby and Alfie were alarmed by Mum's reaction.

"But Mum," they explained. "We just wanted to show you how very much we love you."

They ran towards Mum with tears in their eyes. But Mum's face changed to anger and they backed away.

"Get up those stairs!" bellowed Mum.

Confused and crying, Ruby and Alfie hastily took to their rooms.

Mum forced herself to look at the soggy sandcastle as it dripped and slumped across the newly laid carpet. Also confused and crying, she collapsed onto a chair.

Dave jumped up to snuggle Mum as she sobbed. He hated to see any of his humans feeling unhappy. "This has gone really, really badly," he thought to himself. "It's time for me to sort it out."

Working his unusual magic, Dave scratched his ear. He turned back time to when the twins were showing Mum their sandcastle. This time, things would be very different.

"What have you done?!" howled Mum in despair.

Ruby and Alfie were alarmed by Mum's reaction. They ran towards Mum with tears in their eyes. "We just wanted to show you how very much we love you," Ruby explained.

The twins hugged Mum super tight. "Yeah," Alfie chimed in. "We love you so much and we wanted to show you by giving you the very best thing that we can do."

"And the best thing we can do is build a sandcastle," said Ruby quietly and gesturing toward the now sagging heap of sand.

In almost a whisper, Alfie added, "It's raining and we knew you'd definitely see our sandcastle if we built it inside."

Mum went very quiet for what felt like hours. She wrestled with her emotions while she thought carefully about what to say next. Dave tried to encourage her with his wise eyes.

Finally, sitting Ruby and Alfie down with her, Mum spoke. "Oh you two. I can really see that you love me so very, very much...

... And... next time... please just take me outside to see your sandcastle... even if it is raining.

Mum took a photo of herself, Ruby, Alfie and the sandcastle to keep on the fridge and show Dad.

When they had cleared up the carpet together, Ruby and Alfie set about making a super sandcastle where it belonged... outside!

Dave lay down on Mum's lap and looked up at her, adoringly.

"Now that's more like it. Well done Mum," he thought.

Hey there grown-ups

You may be wondering why I didn't turn back time to when Ruby and Alfie decided to make their very best sandcastle for Mum. Why didn't I change things so that the sandcastle was never made in the middle of the living room carpet? Well, I shall tell you why...

Ruby and Alfie are children. They haven't got the hang of the many 'dos and dont's' that grown-ups have usually mastered. And why should they? After all, children are true novices in the world. There are so very many ropes to learn and, with you humans, it can take a long, long time.

Ruby and Alfie wanted to express their love for their Mum. OK, the method they chose wasn't wise, but they are children; children aren't wise! Children make all sorts of mess-ups as they navigate their way through growing up. It's up to you grown-ups to adjust your responses and behaviours, in order to help the kids navigate and learn.

On the first time around, Mum had a complete (and understandable) knee-jerk reaction. All she could see was her ruined carpet and all the mess. She launched into action without thinking. Mum was upset, the twins were upset and I was upset! The whole thing was a lose-lose.

On the second time around, Mum, while still dismayed at the state of the carpet, took a step back and thought wider than just what was in front of her. She took a moment to think about Ruby and Alfie, considering their motives and how things would have been logical to them. The message about not building sandcastles inside was much clearer on the second time around because there was no anger and upset involved. At the same time, Ruby and Alfie's core message behind their actions was acknowledged. Also, in future, the twins will make wiser decisions. The second time around was a win-win.

About the author

Hil was born in Preston, Lancashire not quite "when God were a lad." Most mornings, you'll find Hil running her spaniels and power walking.

Throughout her time on Earth, she has had an unfailing passion for, and delight in, people, creativity, the wonders of the creative mind and keeping 'shiny'.

Story and metaphor have always been Hil's natural means of connecting with others and she finds them powerful tools for learning and high quality communication, as well as sheer entertainment.

About the illustrator

Stuart Catterson is a life long self taught artist. An artist who loves to have a go at any and all creative processes and styles, from oil painting and etching, to computer art.

Lightning Source UK Ltd.
Milton Keynes UK
UKHW050423200122
397433UK00002B/40

9 780957 191181